Halchita Red

Paige Buffington

Halchita Red
Paige Buffington, 2024

Books may be purchased in quantity and/or special sales by contacting the publisher. All inquiries related to such matters should be addressed to:

Middle Creek Publishing & Audio 9161 Pueblo Mountain Park Road Beulah, CO 81023
editor@middlecreekpublishing.com
(719) 369-9050

First Paperback Edition, 2024
ISBN: 978-1-957483-30-6
Cover Art: AuthoLab Licensed Image, modified and redesigned by David Martin, Middle Creek Publishing & Audio.

Cover Design: David Anthony Martin, Middle Creek Publishing & Audio.

Author Image Credit:
Lyrics from the song "Wildwood Flowers" written by Maude Irving

Halchita Red

Paige Buffington

Middle Creek Publishing & Audio
Beulah, CO   USA

To my most deeply loved relatives.

To Red Willow Valley, our home, and our stories.

CONTENTS

Oh, I'll twine my mingles and my waving black hair.

—from "Wildwood Flowers"

Halchita Red

From 20 Miles Outside of Gallup, Holbrook, Winslow, Farmington, or Albuquerque

1962

Under a sky purpling at dusk, the children paused on the porch of a turquoise, plyboard-patched house. They ran toward the edge where blue pines grew. They brought their fingertips to their thumbs, held their hand-binoculars up to their eyes, looked from the summit they called their summer home and into the distance. For the first time, they noticed beads of lights glittering, ember-like, on the black horizon.

The older relatives sat on the dirt-packed floor; each took turns speaking to the children: *Avoid that place. Shiny things make us go crazy. What will happen if we lose you? If we forget how to talk to each other? What will happen if rainwater comes flooding in? If its foamy backbone carries you away?*

The children nodded, listened. They continued to climb cottonwoods, old sheds corralling their brightly painted home. They lit flashlights under lint-speckled blankets, snuck puppies in through the window, took turns listing the dreams they would bring back home: a truck, a Quarter Horse, a light switch for every room. They listed and laughed until sleep took them—above them, the sparkling Pleiades. Below them, a cornmeal-dusted floor.

Still, they watched the lights, took in how they were expanding. The gleaming highlighted their eyelashes, dust-colored from years spent running under a desert's silver-dollar sun. Neon radiated in the rain-soaked hair hanging down their backs. Breezes lifted the sheets covering the windows, wove into the fibers of their pillows, the tiny spaces between their toes. Someone or something whispered to them,
Come. Come.

The years passed. The children grew.

Some of them stayed and learned winter stories, where to find baby jars filled with golden pollen. They learned to shoot and fight— unafraid to tangle with unnamed things in the dark. Others learned to pack. They left by trains, some by trucks or on foot—all enchanted by the glimmering distance. Some came back with dog tags, shortened hair and broken hearts, spent most of their time listening to music in cars or near the corrals. Others came back with coffee cups printed with seashells and the skylines of cities, their own stories of schools, love, and machines. Some seemingly lived forever among the fire-like lights.

Still, the grandmothers woke before the sun. They took each baby, new, perfect, and unnamed toward the sterling light that stretched from edge to edge. They brought each tiny head with hair soft and black as feathers to their cheeks and whispered, *Shiyazhi, Shiawéé'*. They blessed them with water collected from the cloud-colored confluence below Cameron, the July rains. They called them what they wished for them, what they will always wish for them: *To Return from War, Sunflower, Bluebird, Home.*

Polaroid

Hey. Thought you should know R.J. passed.

Sorry to hear from you in this way. You okay? Do you need to call?

No. They've allowed me leave. I'll be coming through town. Putting down R.J.'s horse for him. Don't really want to run into anyone.

Breakfast at midnight?

He sits across from me, inches closer to the dew-beaded window, stretches his legs across the tattered teal vinyl of this old Route 66 restaurant booth, runs calloused fingertips through freshly service-shortened hair. He motions for me to order first with a nod toward the ground, runs his palms together as if in prayer, slides the grease-stained paper menu over to the waitress.

Pancakes, a cup of fruit, water please.

Coffee.

That's it?

I'm not that hungry. The weather—I shouldn't have come.

You didn't have to stop.

They had no one else to do it.

They would've found someone.

It should've been me. Some days, I can't believe I made it. I can't believe I'm still here.

He lowers his head, stares at the muddied linoleum when I reply, *You know better than to say things like that.* The clearing of his throat. The looking up at me, then, with warworn, familiar eyes. The deep brown of them always knew how to call me back—back to this restaurant, back to the screen of my phone, back to the backmost room of that trailer just outside of Chinle. I had to get back to Gallup for work in the morning, but work is work and he was there and smiling, the world so still and it was snowing. All that glittering we were mesmerized by it—standing cliffside and looking down at Spider Rock, how we stayed so long the silver clouds came down to cover the towering red of it. He said—

My brother would climb it if he could. He wasn't scared of nothing.

They've called me back into an old truck, back to the post office to check for updates, back to the school's library to check my email, to type out letters instead of poems—

Everyone's okay. We miss you. Counting down the days.

They always knew how to make me stretch over the backseats of cars, over coffee or whiskey-ringed tables like this one to put my hands on his heart, have taught me the ways to move them up his weather-worn face. They tell me what he can't say—no talking until the old song coming through the speakers is over, that it's been years since his last slow dance, that he feels older than 31, that there's this ache in his chest when he uses YouTube to relearn colors in our language.

So, another four years. What are your plans?

He says that all he is sure of is this—that the horse knew it would take R.J. into the next world, the reverent way it almost bowed as he loaded the rifle. I notice the shift in his body as we sit in pink and honey neon light caught in the condensation of the old diner's window, listen as the backpacked men come in to ask if anyone is heading north on 491—

We're trying to get to back home. We have grandkids in Monticello, a hundred rodeos to get to, a hundred horses to break. The herds run wild and apparition-like down from the cloud-covered mesas. Thundering to the east, south, west, and north of us.

He studies the rippling in his coffee, a waiter drops a hill of plates, he squeezes his eyes, fists as if waiting for impact—

My oldest and wildest love, come back to me.

Tell me how the coffee is, how you know the waitress, retell the stories you shared on the long drives into the cactus and boulder speckled valley of Arizona when we were newly twenty, beautiful, pinning Polaroids of ourselves to the roof of whatever car was running well enough to make it. Tell me, again, who brought down stars to give those silver and knowing eyes to horses. Name the relative whose younger self lives, handsome and strong, in the black and white backgrounds of old westerns.

Remind me how Searchlight *was the only English word he knew.*

I notice him looking for and taking note of all the exits, how his eyes examine each stranger coming in. He rests his head in his hands.

Come back to me—list the names of the relatives your mother left you and your brother with because she wanted to be young and free in the dance halls of Albuquerque, how she always dreamt of apartment living. You were nearly walking, your little brother so new, wrapped and sleeping near the woodstove. Tell me the name of that wildfire. Remind me how they said the elk looked as they ran down from the mountain and away from it, red comets stretching from what was left of their velvet crowns. Remind me how, 200 miles away but on the same night that the animals ran down, burning, from the summit, your mother walked away from a night out and a rollover with only a burn on her right wrist. Tell me how your relatives always said those animals gave themselves to keep her here, to bring her home. List every name I've heard you call that night, that burn—a lesson, sobriety, a homecoming, a shelled supernova, a butterfly.

Break this stretch of sky in half, break the whole world apart. Let's watch the swans bring snow down from the north, refill the reservoirs. Sing the lyrics from your new favorite songs, tell me your creation stories. Tell how your grandpa drove 500 miles north with an infant to take him to the headwaters of the Colorado, that it was lightly snowing when grandpa splashed whitewater across your little brother's new face and feet, how, from that point on, your brother dreamt and spoke in mountains, that his name was the first your grandfather would call out to in evenings, how your grandmothers could spot him by the turkey vultures circling above or the dust he'd kick up running home. List all the places your *tsili* would look for your grandfather after old age took him: a plowed line in the cornfield, the back booth of a downtown bar, the streets of Gallup, a red horse running in a foot of snow.

He doesn't talk about the vultures, his grandfather, or mother. Instead, he lists the ways our mountains are like the mountains in the Middle East, describes how shrapnel splits the insides of a muscled horse, a soldier's back. He mentions the friend in high school who lived up near the red rocks on the east side of town, stands to show me how this friend walked out onto the tracks just behind the motels, recants the conductor's statement about how he tried to slow the train, describe the steadiness with which the teenager stood on the tracks, eyes tightly closed, open-mouthed as if screaming, palms covering his ears. He guesses what this friend might have been listening to his last five minutes on this plane, something poem-like with heavy guitars, uses a dusty napkin to write what was written in marker across the last shirt he chose to wear, a plain white t-shirt stained with an amber dust.

I think it was the only way he could think of to get out of this place. I wish he joined with me.

Let's talk about something else—standing beneath runoff in spring, the songs you can play on the harmonica, each color your mother painted the house of your childhood—a salmon, aquamarine, canary box in that treeless valley of an iron red.

Tell me the names of your favorite dogs, the nicknames for all your cousins.

Map out the latitude and longitude of your father's mint-green home in out-there, Arizona, your landmarks, the juniper half dead or half alive, the boulder dotted with shelled fossils. Show me how you twisted wire to close the gate, where you tied balloons around trees so that relatives could find the cookout, how these fence lines always helped you find your way home.

I have nothing to say that you don't already know.

My love, you can teach us how to unravel. Teach us how to go years without calling, how to live with a heart emptying at news that another elder has left. Teach us how you go days without sleeping and drive thousands of miles while wide awake. Tell us everything we've always known: It was all written for us, that all of this was always meant to be—

I can't sleep- might not be able to write for a few days. Can I tell you something? You always ask why I joined. I guess there's a lot of time to think out here. I'm thinking about my brother. I wonder where he slept. Did you know I spent years knocking on the doors of so many houses? I remember watching headlights move across our ceiling. Every time hoping it was him. I looked under the caps of every man walking in town. Years. I had old VHS tapes of Christmases, first-laugh parties playing nonstop. I started dreaming of him and grandpa. They were speaking that old Navajo. They were on cinnamon horses. It was like it was in outer space, like Saturn or some shit. It was lightly snowing there.

He says these dreams bloomed and knotted in his stomach, his heart. I imagine nightmares crawling into his shoes, between the dusty envelopes in his glovebox, his textbooks. *I can't stay.* He found a place where others could beat the prickling out of his body, rewire his mind. He left for South Carolina, a First Duty Station, soon after, Anbar, other placed dotted with date palms. Even after years, he and his mother spent nights anticipating a knock on the door, a midnight phone call, a confirmation of what his dreams had been telling him, of what both of their hearts had already known.

Still, the flashing lights startled his mother. It was late November, the first days of a two-week leave, nearly six, and already dark. She dropped the freshly peeled potato on the linoleum floor. Shavings of sterling silver, loose beads, mud tracked in two seasons ago stuck to the wet white of it. She rinsed and kept scrubbing, said it was still good. *I want to have food ready for my sons.* He was and had been the only son sitting at the table for years. It was raining and neither of them were hungry. She sat at the table, thumbed her scarred wrist, her signal of nervousness, said that he had to be the one to look, to ask them inside for coffee. The uniformed men wrapped yellow tape around clouds of grey sagebrush, looked down into the wash, flashlights illuminated their concentrated faces, searching.

Someone had confessed to something, gave a general location. They had found a duffel, they were thinking something, someone was nearby. The small animals picked at all the soft parts of it —a handkerchief, the tongue, ears, and eyes. Authorities wouldn't confirm it was human or release a name for a few weeks, maybe months, years. By then he'd be away again, outside of some city in a desert I'll never see, armed on a mud wall, writing out a postcard.

He almost made it home.

Tell me why you think we cannot bring ourselves to wipe all this steam off the windows to see clearer. Remind me that it hurts so much, that we will never really look through. He says, *They never have warm coffee in this place. He would always say that, that he would go young. It should have been me.* He had always planned to leave in the morning. He says he forgot and can't find anyone who remembers the Navajo name for this place, wonders what his great-grandpa would think of all this— the lights, how we talk through machines, how we never truly rest.

He's leaning into it, re-enlisting. Maybe he'll go back to school after the next four years are over—Boston, New York, D.C., somewhere without a mesa, constellation, or a dirt road in sight. He doesn't know why he stops when driving through at all, that he wishes he could come and leave quietly like snow.

The Men in Your Family

My grandfather drew a shaky line in a deep, January snow.

Shi'tsoi, there is this line that is drawn for each of us when we are born.
We won't go past the end of our line. We watched the sky adjust herself to the sun's light, the black shifting into indigo, then gold. We silently acknowledged his trembling hands, a small pain below the heart, the fact that snow can hide where earth's horizon ends—how easy it can be to get sick, to step off the edge of this world, to disappear.

He passed suddenly that summer. Since, I've never returned to the place he drew the line. I've learned that some of us choose to walk our lines backwards, that some of us choose to stretch them.

Sometimes, our lines are stretched around the wood pallet fence lining the homestead and we grow up giving names to babies and to horses. Sometimes, the lines are the yellow center lines of roads leading to Sanders or Farmington, to the frequented front porch of a lounge, to a heavy love for neon, for glittery things. Sometimes, the line wraps around a linoleum-floored kitchen, an old woodstove's rust-brown edge. Grandma lingered around grease splatter decades dry, always had some potatoes going, eggs frying for the babies, plates kept warm in the oven for her wandering sons.

Twenty or a hundred miles from home, the sons stuck their thumbs toward a searing sun. All up and down Highway 491, they tried to make it home from the night, the rodeo season, the year. How time flew dropping coins into jukeboxes clicking with crystal chandelier country. How easy it was to lose track of time when lines wrapped around the Route 66 hotels like barbwire, when a couple weeks in the neon lights, in the cigarette clouds, calmed the humming hooves left rolling around their ribcages, bruised purple and blue like galaxies they camped beneath. Time slipped when two-stepping helped them forget the months, the names of daughters they left at home—

The girls' lines were the bottoms of their grandmother's skirts. They sat in their circumferences learning colors, memorizing place names, *Pollen Mountain* and *Shattered House*, what you say to spiders before you kill them—

I'm sorry you have no family here, bartenders told the men when they stayed too long, when they pointed to pictures of Torreon or Shiprock legends riding crazed and bucking bulls, when hours passed, and they became storytellers. *He was like a father to me, that cowboy right there. He punched a bull between the eyes for being stubborn. You know that bull kicked him all the way into the eighth world.*

Black-eyed and beaten, the sons paid their nephews, their younger cousins or relatives to drive them from bar to bar, the fifty miles from Chambers to Zuni, from Milan to Gallup. They promised them a case of pop and a picture show in Gallup as a payment, the long roads promised the young men time away from the homestead. At the rodeos, they made and spent four-hundred dollars—*All in one day*, grandma said, *I chased the sheep back into the fence, they were scattered all over the pass. I went into town to sell the strands of beads I strung. I watched young mothers walk out of stores with boxes of cereal, gallons of milk. I wonder if they counted stars when they were pregnant, all those babies and not one father walked through that door.*

So young I learned the names of neon colors—electric lime, proton, chartreuse. So young I learned to not turn pages backwards, to turn back when a snake crosses my path. So young the boys memorized the rodeo announcer route, the turns in the road starting in the red of Ganado and ending at the grey base of First Mesa.

There, sisters crack blue paper bread in their kitchen, talk of the last time they saw their brother. Maybe he was arrested in Flagstaff. Maybe he ran off with a white woman. Maybe his line led him off the edge of this world.

All-American Biography

Illiterate, the coal-faced boy lured foals into abandoned trailers with matchlight and prayer. Come, First Horse, Maria de Soledad. His mother showed him how to call to them, how she slept in the glass-littered ditches outside Farmington and Holbrook. Stretching barbwire-torn flannel like wings over her weathered body, she let snows gather on her pregnant belly. Frost webbing over his jeans. Then snow piling in his crying mouth. How cold gave him a light complexion.

The things he did when she left him. He arranged blackened bones of dead horses into mother-shapes like song. Gallons of gasoline outside the door. Flowers pushing themselves through snow.

Clouds gathering thick in his lungs. Frost on a crow's swollen body. The flannel she left still full with the shape of her. The way she moved walking into town. The sway she moved with when she taught him to walk. The way gasoline softens snow. The shape horses take when they're set on fire.

At Mention of Moab

Dad sleeps in a fish-tin trailer. Fifty miles inside Utah state lines, diesels

hum, split his spring-filled, rusting canteens. The restless highway winds wake the pages of a dusty bedside bible, tear worn maps taped across the aluminum walls. His fingertips know the textures of rising paper mountains, the mesas, the thin blue lines of canyon rivers—but wading waist-deep in their shimmering worlds is something he has always struggled to understand.

The insides of his lightless apartment once held our favorite landscapes—the horizon of a mattress, the curve of a canteen, a coffee cup. We sat in a rust-ringed bathtub, wrapped our arms around legs, hands around flashlights, we stayed warm together. Dad pulled the knife from his pocket, cut the carnival glowsticks in two, splattered their contents on the walls, created neon constellations. We loved the nights on nights like these—tracing the ghost tails of meteors, the telescopes, our hair unbraided and shining.

Girls, one day, I'll go on a trip alone.

For years, we left prayers around his tire rims, on the barrel of the Winchester he kept beside the bed, inside the envelopes stacked in his glovebox. We took his words into fists, blew them to the north. *This is what I'll do, I will go to Arizona or Colorado. It will be late, dark, and I'll swerve*

into the other lane. My ashes should be placed on a mountain in Wyoming, or mixed with gunpowder, be sure to hold the rifle like I taught you— and this is where we stopped listening.

No hot water this morning or yesterday morning. Small, cold mountains rose on our skins. She'd ask, *What burns longer, hotter? Cedar or pitch? One day, we won't be here when you don't know what to do or say*—I can't answer when dad asks if I remember hiding in the bottom of her skirt, crying after her, if I want a beer when he talks about the man who fell asleep on the train tracks, lists where police found his leg and arms, beside a pine, beneath the hood of a broken down car I asked, *Where did you find his heart?* He said, *Like most men, I don't think he had one to lose.*

But I remember the pattern of his heartbeat when he ran behind me on that fourth morning. We ran with hungry dogs, struggled for miles in spring cold. I watched for sun, the quiet way it pulls the purple horizon from the dark, listened for the hooves separating snow, the envelopes full of prayers opening—*Be careful. But keep going.*

Grandma asked him to bring a truckload of wood, to run, to yell into the morning to call everything holy to us. Every few steps he yelled into the dark and we may not have beat the sun, but we made it home, oh yes, we made it home.

January 31, 1991

She woke in the belly of a border town night. Soft snow shifted over quiet sidewalks. Winter stars scattered in constellation-forms. The insides of her hands rested warm on a swollen tummy.

Eight-thousand miles from her lowered eyelids, from the fingerprinted glass of water collecting dust on her nightstand, a bomb shattered the breath that bridged a man to a woman whose ribcage stretched over his heart like wings expanding in winter light. They slept inches and dream-worlds apart. *One thousand one. One thousand two.* He trapped himself in a dream of his father's wind-worn skin and cigar-stained teeth.

His ghost smoked in a rust-tinged car that began to shake, shake until he pointed. They watched the sun explode. Light bloomed behind eyelids, curtains. Heat spilled into the paper room. *Open.*

Calloused thumbs traced a newborn's mouth. They waited to see their reflections swim in the black seas of her new eyes, to unfold her hands like tiny maps. She yawned. Jets cracked early-morning clouds. Prayers ran through engines. A boy in California dreamt that every animal on Earth had died. A war played on every station.

An older relative went searching for the cows. He never liked hospitals, machines made him ache between his lungs, and stayed behind. He waited for the new-one at home as those who went to see her wiped washboard dust off their shoes, their faces. Everyone took turns opening her hands. *Open your hands, stretch, open for all the world to come crawling.*

Reckless

and twenty in a hotel with a shimmering pool.
I count the white and blue-striped umbrellas circling
the turquoise of it,
hear the singing slot machines downstairs.

For a hundred dollars more, the comforters are still fat with feathers.
High-ceilinged and freshly painted with eggshell or blush the
bloodstains, ghosts are hidden a little better than they are in
the black mold motels just off Route 66, I-40.

Still, I have dreams of fights that happened in this room,
sense that this bed is a bed someone took their last breath on.
Maybe they, too, stared at the twin paintings of Gila
Monsters, counted the black and orange beads on their slick,
shining bodies while they waited for their love, just back from
bootcamp, to bring them coffee just before falling asleep and
never waking up again.

Or maybe what I'm feeling is the energy left by a child.

I imagine her at 5 a.m., holding her breath and examining the stilled body of her grandmother,
finally exhaling when the great, quilt-adorned hill of her elder rises and falls
with a deep breath.

I'm young and can still dismiss thoughts of death and sickness, can fall asleep quickly.

I think, *All my loves are here and will be here forever.*

I shouldn't think like this.

It will all work out in the end.

I'm young and believe that an $800 paycheck is all we need, that a weekend to ourselves in this hotel, him going to get me coffee or learning how to play a sweet song on the guitar and asking me to sing means

something—

that I can play this recording of our late-night duet on a tough night fifteen years from now and say to myself,
Look at how he looked at me.

In sickness and in health.

Look at how young we were.

Look at all the love that was there.

In this dimly-lit future, I see myself teary-eyed, in cell phone
light, beneath a comforter.
My body, softened with children, shaking.
I stop the recording somewhere in the middle.

I carry and place our sleeping children in their car seats, start
the SUV—

headlights uncover miles of dirt road, of desert.
I slow with the windows down, listen for him crying out for
his brother, my eyes always searching for him,
dressed in all black, almost invisible in
our sagebrush-dotted slice of the world.

Reckless in the backseat, the cigarette-burnt front seat,

the tailgate where the bottles and the gold bubbling in them

captured firelight from a New Year's Eve bonfire,

moonlight reflecting and almost blue in snow.

In all this brightness he said,

I can't wait to get out of here.

And later, *Don't wait for me.*

And much later, *I miss my brother. Just stay the night.*

So young with a smile like the Milky Way, shining and so close

we thought we could

climb

the red rocks towering all around us and walk out onto it.

The brilliance of all of it—the pinon-pitch fire blazing, being

nineteen, the coyote-scattered constellations and the thought

of us using them as

sterling bridges reminded me of a neon strip in the desert

near Holbrook,

camping in the sage, maroon, bone-white striped hills

somewhere near there—

how the cashier of the gas station where we bought

cigarettes, water had

the same stained hands, yellowing mustache

of the operator of that rusted Ferris Wheel in Santa Monica,

where you asked how many kids I want,

if I thought I could live in tree-covered Georgia, below the

steel mountains in Bavaria, how many others

I'd meet if I ever went

to write

in Santa Fe.

This operator had the same song playing from a handheld

radio as the manager of the motel in Abilene or Temple or

somewhere in that sweltering state where we stayed in—

cigarette smoke spiraling,

blinds drawn,

belly to belly,

the green, blue, purple neon sign humming,

singing every lyric from the shuffled playlist.

We couldn't tell

night from day,

desert from plain.

The roads in El Paso looked the same as those in Abilene did

those weeks we spent packing, days so blistering the heat

rippled off the earth.

We threw his boxes on a flatbed and we headed

for Truth or Consequences, Albuquerque, Gallup—

to the couch in the studio, the mattress on the floor

where months later, I would wait

for the trees of Fort Jackson,

the dust-covered buildings between the Tigris and Euphrates

to be through with him.

Three years later, I would be in Santa Fe,

between the lines of poems and speculative fiction, waiting

for his first child to arrive.

I would look at the pictures of the new baby,

rosy-cheeked and perfect,

the mother glowing

like a sun and I'd tell myself—

He chose. That's enough.

Your children are taller than me, now.

I ran into them around Thanksgiving on a last-minute trip to

the store for eggs.

I thought of the afternoon I turned every burner of the stove

on—

letters from Iraq, Texas, turning

to black flakes, snowing around the tiny kitchen, onto my hair.

I'd spent hours sweeping, ridding the tiles and myself of them

so that I wouldn't keep parts of you in my room, in the chambers

of my body.

Still, one of your jackets, the one with tiny gold rifles pinned to

denim, hangs

in the closet.

Still, I remember that I left my grandma and uncle

—both gone, now—

dipping eggs into pink and yellow dyes on Easter Sunday

to go on a

drive to somewhere and end up in a tent

just off the coast

with you— how,

noticing your smile had changed, I let you run into the ocean

fog by yourself and waited in a car

for hours.

Still, I remember how, months later, you would be at my door

on Christmas Eve,

last-minute granted leave and a surprise flight, a shoe-game

and gift exchange

with your family.

You'd drop me off early that night only to never

pick me back up again.

Still, all these years later, I smile at the thought of Texas,

read old novels about the horse-covered plain and sometimes

see us young, sleeping in all that soft yellow,

the sounds of horses lulling

us to sleep.

Still, I would smile that Easter Sunday,

your steady and confident knock on the door.

I think of how the ocean spray must have felt on your face after

months of gunfire and dry sand.

In a dream, I tell my uncle and grandmother to pack

their best clothes— the four of us walk into the water,

hold onto each other for balance,

laugh as we let the water crash into our hearts.

Sometimes, I am afraid of sleep.

I think of how my mom found my grandmother,

curled up in blankets

as if in deep rest.

I imagine how hard she must have shaken her,

first in frustration,
then in disbelief.
Still, she sometimes says, *If I had left work earlier in the morning to
check on her*—

The ocean is 665 miles to the West, recklessly throwing
itself into the slick, rocky shores as it will for eons after us.
Tsetah Dibe sparkles in the sky to the East of me.

In a letter that I later gave to the fire, you wrote

I can't sleep,

left your bunk and walked, bootless, into winter to feel
something.

You needed a sign from anyone or anything from home.

It was faint at first, then a heartbeat, a pulsing wave of silver, a
breath, a cluster of one thousand stars.
You found it.

Even in that desert on the other side of the world,
even with loss and your hardened demeanor and all the new
places you have slept
and yellow fields burning,
even with horses running off of cliffs
and bombs vibrating in your chest and

all that time passing—

it was there.

Sites: A Poem in Three Parts

Route 11

Hills rise and roll, brown and lonely like the saddle the family's oldest uncle left. We are nearing the bullet-holed road signs, the scripture-inscribed walls of the old store where the wandering or heartbroken danced, shoved their palms into the chests of those they loved or were up against.

This is the wash where relatives took the mattresses of the dead or dying to burn—where cousins gathered to shoot bottles, old dishes, the dogs that killed four sheep.

This is also the sisters' place.

This is where the girls stopped their bikes to listen for shots, to watch cottontails scatter and kick up casings, to watch the smoke and dirt rise until it consumed the crows, covered a rising moon—

But look to see the palominos running, grass-stained and wild into the wash, back out and up. Watch your hands now tracing their sun-white tails, following them like cornfield birds.

We are here, the rusted Mustang marks a churchyard, the deer tracks, a holy place. This was once their home, before the windows were boarded up, the woodstove stolen—a home with coffee boiling, a quilt-covered couch, quail climbing woodpiles with black crowns shining.

Place your ear to the door like a shell—listen to laughter, watch them unbraid hair fragrant with dirt, or cedar, or both, black hair gathering, rivering in the water of a silver tub.

Watch a grandmother chase the girls out to run, tell them to not come home until the sky goes purple or pink, to cover their handprints, to not look back—

Watch them race hand in hand to the cornfield—a moonrise reflecting in the bellies of the dark horses, in the girls' hair, undone.

From The Lower Rio Grande

The Rio Grande carries the grey, wet skeletons of trees, a child's shoe. Watch the water, muddied and angry, weave its way around a rusted dryer.

Watch the left-behind sister turn under August clouds, swollen with monsoon rain. Help her list their names in the river sand, the constellations, the names of mountains, the horses hand-printed with mud. Place your mouth to the cold, watered earth. Help her remember the taste of the cornfield she called a church.

Walk her into the water as she tells you about how a cowboy pushed her out of and then against his truck, how she ran from him then walked four miles back into town but how this thought, the song that was playing on the radio still doesn't split her heart as much as when she thinks about all her sister left her with—how they pretended to be astronauts, how they used a thrown-out dryer as a spaceship, how a late September rain once flooded the house, how her sister rode her bike into the cloudburst, how she lost her shape as she faded into the road, how this was the first time her sister left her barefoot and crying on the porch, *Come back* escaping her mouth like a prayer.

Albuquerque

The grandparents parked between Village Inn and Motel 6, the sisters slow danced beneath cottonwood leaves, golden and mixed with snow. The grandmother marked one sister's socks, jeans, and shoes with permanent marker. The left-behind took in the shape of the initials.

They stood knee-deep in the low, brown river, walked until the waterline touched ribcages, their hearts. Grandma scolded the one left behind, *It is not good to cry after people.* Watch her watch the road for miles, close her eyes somewhere between Laguna and her home.

Watch how the years go by—more mattresses burn, watch men board up the store, listen to the songs of birthdays, new songs of love. Watch one sister crawl out of a boarding school window, apply lipstick as she goes into downtown Albuquerque or further south. Watch her walk into the backrooms of trailers. Hear the car honking when she calls from payphones, *I finally left. Can you send me money? I'll find my way home.*

Watch the herd of palomino grow in numbers, grow wild. Listen to the firewood crack in the stove. Take note of the silence when the one left behind traces the initials tattooed inside her wrist, tells the grandmother, *I heard from my sister.* Watch the grandmother's eyes look down to the floor, to her shoes, the tops of her white socks brushing the bottom of a bird-printed skirt.

Follow the one left behind into a canyon, white and yellow rocks towering to the left and right. The girls found deer tracks in this place once, drew hearts around them but never walked deep enough to find the herd— Listen to the left behind tap a bottle, list her maybes. Maybe she's smoking a cigarette right now in the belly of a city, Tucson, or San Francisco, maybe. Maybe that was her my uncles saw. Maybe she's walking near the ridgeline, watching the palominos running, grass stained and wild, tracing their shell-white tails. Maybe her hair is still midnight-black and rivering. Maybe she found a fawn. Maybe it's curled, almost sleeping, her singing the names of mountains, naming the stars scattered on its back.

Because You Are Magic, I Refuse to Admit the Last Place I Saw Her

was in the parking lot of a Costco, just off of I-25
in Albuquerque, the Q, Burque.
It was in October, when the leaves are dead or dying, when the
Rio Grande
exposes its mud-colored backbone to the freeways, the
dimming sun.
It was in this half-time, in half-light, when the grey cranes
move down to El Paso, Miami, maybe, or somewhere I can't
name, somewhere
deeper south.

Her, in the backseat, best beads and a flower-printed skirt,
feet resting on a rusting metal milk crate, said she couldn't see
the flock, asked me to tie her shoes as I had been doing since
I was six, to pull the net over paper plates towering in the
truck bed, asked if I wanted the leftover breadsticks for my
drive back up to Santa Fe.

Some nights I wonder if she saw the faint line of the several
winged bodies,

if she chose not to acknowledge the pain just below her heart,
her lost sons,

if she chose not to watch their silent, grey migration. I
wonder if she hears me call Olive Garden a sacred place—
watches me throw it roses, carnations and knitting needles
from I-25,

if she watches me bow my head each time
I crawl up a truck's bed
as if entering a ceremony, a mud-floored church.

At times, I wonder if she can feel this hymn of wind-filled
plastic bags,

this shallow river swelling in my throat.

Away From Home

Children run in Nike Airs, Converse or barefoot, shatter the
shelled backbones of dry washes, skeletons of diseased cattle.
This is where you are,

where you asked Grandpa the names for crazy people, what
happened to the newborn twins left alone in the car. They're
buried in cornfield brush you see where the earth was broken
from where you are.

The trailer in Pinedale is sun-faded, abandoned now. You slept
beside dogs beneath the truck camper, nobody checked or
asked where you are. Do they still ask? Where you are,

or where you wish you were now, black horses run until we
mistake their rumble for monsoons, manes tangle in electricity
lines, children tiptoe to touch coal hooves. Death spins like
ornaments along highways where you are,

snow covers the New Mexico/Arizona stateline. Young men
shoot horses, two hundred dollars a head. The babies need

food and diapers. Trailers filled with broken hearts from where
you are,

You still see *Cheii* watch deer shake first snow of their ears, still
hear his sisters say, *I wish he didn't eat sweets, potatoes so much. You
know, he always asked where you are.*

For years, you've been walking counterclockwise through
homes, trying to remember what to say when you brush your
hair at night, look for hanging chains of basketball hoops close
to where you are.

You once shook the hand of the man who named the holy skin
behind the ear. Is this the word for planet or that sacred, soft
skin? Paige, you can't remember from where you are.

To Return after The War or Wars

I.

We can meet in late May or early June.

I've thought about the silver sun swimming in your Wayfarers, shining in the century-old sterling wrapped around your wrists—your playlists, the small or swelling aches we all carry. I've thought of your father in thunderstorms, under a coffee-ringed table, rocking back and forth in his own embrace. I've prayed to rid him of the things that crawled into his boots and followed him back from jungles 8,000 miles away, thought of how they might have found their way into your brother's pockets, caused him to also walk off. I've remembered my father and his weakening father, barefoot and toes touching, celebrating under runoff in Escalante after a decade without a heavy rain and apart—I've thought about our feet.

I've imagined our bodies, cool, in jade pools just off Lake Powell. Shiny-feathered condors with their candy-red heads, a deep vermillion—these are all dreams of you—forever in an old pickup, a handheld radio, young, a backwards cap, headphones in your ears in the years before your service, the whole world stretched out before you again.

You frame a rust landscape in a rectangle made by your hands. You turn toward me, my hair still heavy and dripping with lake, bring my face to yours. Yours and your father's dog tags swing from your neck, all rust and grooved by your thumb. The sun, now a red and rippling yolk, slips off the sandstone's darkened edge and leaves for the other side of the world.

II.

I bought four new tires, dry cleaned a favorite rose colored dress.

The man who has loved me since junior high checked the clicking in the engine, replaced my taillight. He drove it up and over the hill to check the transmission, cleaned and vacuumed the inside, shrugged when I asked if it will be okay for a long trip, said *Should be. Take the back roads. Go through Hopi,* asked me to stay awhile, to have a cup of coffee with his father. Stained hands, a mountain in the distance, coal-less and flattened, cans of air duster in the corners, grinds collecting at the bottom of my cup.

They told me the well's been dry since I left thirteen years ago, asked me where I've been and where I plan on going, why I came back, what it means that an old owl comes to sit on their peach tree every evening, its sound pulsing into the night. *What does it mean when the peaches never come out sweet?*

Oil-covered hands wrapped around a cup, enamel chipping. Gasoline, old bicycles, a dog and its ribcage, the same martial arts movie playing, muted, on an old t.v.

The battery-powered radio played into the evening. Father and son sat with their eyes closed, sang, laughed, and coughed. We heard that old song that tells of a burning—the one where the man with a voice as silver as your bracelet sings out the story of submitting to love, watches fire take everything around him. I stayed through the coughing, ignored the brown bloodstains like star-scatter on the table, watched as a father kicked out a chair from beneath his son, told him to start a fire.

I followed the son, shoulders slouching, head down, a walk I've known since I was fourteen. I held his face near the woodpile, sat through the old, swaying hurt, stacked wood carefully in his arms. I watched him shred papers, stack splinters of pine carefully in a potbellied stove. He wiped his nose with a tattered sleeve, a small flame rippled in his eyes. He listed the ways his life would be different if I had stayed, grabbed at my shoulders and pulled me into his chest. I crawled out from his grip, ran back to my car. I left the crying, the hands being thrown toward the moon, the gunshots in the distance.

My car is ready for the three-hundred miles. Water at our waists, red sand in our hair, our mouths, between our teeth.

III.

I've had this sweet, sweet taste in my mouth, wondered if you've missed the taste of black coffee from a dew-lined Styrofoam cup, a warm corn cake just pulled up from earth, your relatives laughing in the light blue of dawn. I've been daydreaming of the road, window down, my hair long and black, just like an old Elvis song, its like a river in a highway wind. I'm headed West—*Sedona, Las Vegas, Los Angeles,* turning North within a hundred miles of where you were born. A pool of fresh rainwater, white sandstone, cloudburst, water spilling off rock and into the Colorado.

Love, I've had these dreams of you.

I see you playing that pawnshop acoustic guitar in a small house, vibrant against the mudstone. Your father builds a shade, an armful of cottonwood leaves shining, him whole and laughing, he waves up to me. In another, your brother on a bike with training wheels on an endless dirt road, arms out like he's flying. In my favorite, you're in a hallway or a small room lit and smiling, waiting in blue, red, purple jukebox light.

IV.

We've scribbled webs of characters from our favorite folk albums into spiral notebooks. We've climbed ladders to tiptoe and touch constellations. We've jumped into those jade waters from a houseboat. We've listed all the ways we'd come back to help our communities, all of the reasons we want to start at twenty again.

You, critiquing a photo a friend gave to me. You frame it in a rectangle made by your hands. A weathered cowboy leans against an old building under a starry night. A cigarette hangs from his bottom lip. You say it reminds you of your father in his cowboy days, when something as simple as a shiny horse could help him forget the war. I ask you what helps you forget the war. The phone in your pocket rings. You hold your finger up to your lips to quiet me, signaling all this will have to wait for another time. You scribble the names of cities, requirements. Your legs grow restless. It's like you're running in your sleep.

V.

I will call when I cross the state line. I can meet you anywhere under that Arizona sky.

I can take my time if you're not ready. I can leave this old Honda running in the parking lot of an old motel in Flagstaff.

I will listen to the slow song of snow melting and gathering at the base of the abalone-shelled mountain. Snow-water, pines, paper mountain grass, me running my fingers through my hair, glancing down at my phone in the passenger seat.

I'm waiting for it to tell me that you're ready to come home, that you're on a plane flying in.

It's okay if you're hesitant, tired. It's okay if you feel bigger than this place. I can rent a room. We can pretend we are eighteen or eight again when all we wanted was a hotel room with a pool. You can sleep. I can call my father and ask him to tell me about how a family built an underground bunker outside of Holbrook, about where a family of mountain lions travels. I will tell him, *Tell me your best desert stories. Help me help him fall in love with this place again.*

We can pretend we are in the bright colors of a fever dream, that we were given another chance to rewrite our histories, to redirect the tributaries of our lives. We can park the Honda in the empty dirt lot that overlooks the lake. You can take me to the docks to watch the Colorado carve the only landscape we will ever think and write about, the only thing we will ever truly belong to. We can take our shoes off like children. We can dig our feet into the wet sand. We can overturn the rocks belonging to the burrowing animals in evening, stay years or decades to watch our feet become blue or umber, the colors of their bellies, of a damper, cooler earth. We can have this all to ourselves.

Rainbow Bridge, red-tailed hawks, Wayfarers, the sterling in your bracelet, the sun. Tell me when you feel like you can come home from Boston, New York, Chicago, whichever traffic and light-filled place you might be. Come when you feel like you're strong enough to take on the sadness—if you can dance in that hall on Navajo Drive, walk the alley outside of it where your cousin was found, facedown, in a pool of his own blood. Come if you can drive to the Wahweap overlook just to the South where your father's vehicle was found shortly after your mother left, a set of boot prints leading straight to the lake.

Hold this sand in your fists. Watch it fall back into itself by our feet. Take my hand in yours grainy with sediment, take me to water. We wade waist-deep into the lake. Old country songs reach us from the Honda parked near the shore, water skims our ears and jaws.

My love, I can meet you there, late May, early June, when the mudstone is a searing white.

Sun Dagger

I asked you to move your feet. The crows sick with city cried into chuparosa, they called to us from wires. Thin, black strands fell at our feet, into our hair, our hands. You said they were light as fishbone, feathers or tire strands, maybe. You said you could drive one thousand miles without blinking, that you could be a bird. I said, *a bird would see that we are losing light.* It was already fifteen past seven, all lavender with haze. You said, *I know what time it is. All this moving has rubbed my heels raw.* The walking, you said, had ruined your dollar-store flats. You dropped the trash bag full of clothes, of DVDs, hair rollers near the stop sign, sat on a curb warm with the Yuma's cindering sun. *It's time to go back,* I said. *Remember?* You said to give you a minute. It was something. It was always something. When we were younger, it was the birthday song, fear of drowning. Daydreaming and not wanting to haul water. Today, the sun, maybe, the sun and all its shining. Your legs heavy as horses. Traffic, needing a cigarette. Your hair hadn't been washed.

I watched you unweave your braids. You said, *Grandma made them too tight*, I said we wouldn't tell her, we didn't tie your hair back up, we let you run the canyons wild. Dad called you golden-maned, his tiny mouse, let water trickle down your head to ease the white sun's burning. Remember filling milk gallons with spring water, the black pooling at a canyon's mossy bottom, the minnows in their tin suits. The purple landscape we visited abandoned and blazing, left to sidewinders and buzzards, to us under that sky wide-opened, we were almost airless. Dad said, *I feel like I could disappear.* You said, *I want to find the sun dagger.* You wanted to watch a blade of light move and slice a rock-carved spiral in half, to capture a source of light. We traced the chalk-white waterlines with our fingers for miles, looked in every crevice, searched until our toes touched the highway, until the clouds caught fire. We hunted until the sea finally called the sun home.

You hid your pink, sunned face in his collarbone, placed your ear near the pocket by his heart. *Don't cry, baby girl. We will find it next time.* He carried you out, bought a gas-station t-shirt. A horned toad, the light dagger screen-printed, you wore it always. To church and school, receptions, the shooting range. Little, restless animal you paced in that shirt the night dad threw a mattress into his truck camper, you asked me what he was packing for. A rifle, a few books, the tent, his button up shirts, we watched the objects move like the trains. Grandma made us go to bed. *Don't chew on your collar. Leave him be. Don't cry after a man.* Remember? You made me spit out the sleep tea she boiled for us, made me bury the remaining herbs. We snuck out the window, crawled up the tailgate, saw some of what he packed—a few dishes, Tupperware packed with bacon and squash, the baby wipes we used to clean ourselves. So, we climbed into the cave smelling of summer and hid.

We listened to the hum of the highway, counted streetlights, you asked if we were moving west. Dad stopped the truck when he heard voices from the camper. *Goddamn girls. I'm not going all the way back.* Remember? We turned into a Wal-Mart in Winslow, he yelled into the payphone, gave a clerk twenty dollars, she said she'd take care of us until our grandma got there. She held you while you cried, whispered in your ear like it was the day you were born. She taught us how to count to ten in her language, made bologna sandwiches, gave us honey packets for dessert while we waited, you said you were sorry for dreaming. You said you thought dad was taking us back to Canyonlands or to California, you never stopped crying after his truck, but I looked toward the interstate for grandma's car. I was happy to go home.

I pack shoeboxes, plastic bags cloud-like in the backseat, I wait for you to stand. You say the only patterns you remember are those of ditches and how they all lead out of that place we call home, truck stops, your cigarette breaks, how dad always turned left to move further west. You say, *It was easier to move, to crawl into cars with trust. We were much younger; everything was more alive then—*

But you were vibrant once, remember? At birth, the older relatives showed our new bodies to dawn's soft blue and gave us names. They asked us to grow our hair long. Hair snaking in an old bathtub we used as a pool, mine dark like lightning-struck trees, yours the honey we spread over crackers. Remember when we lost our brushes and used our hands as combs. Remember being thrown in morning snow, boiling water over fire, they said all of it would make us strong. We stayed up all night, hung posters of singers on the wall, we became young women. You spun under burning skies, said you wished the whole world had this sky, jumped from railroad tie to railroad tie and asked, *Why would he leave this?* You slept in the corral with the lambs some nights. Remember? You held the books he left up to your nose, fanned the pages, inhaled, but said it didn't hurt, said you never wanted to leave home.

You left some weeks after grandma passed, remember? You met a man from some city, you said he taught you how to grow wings, how to feel good, that it was your time to fly. When all compasses rusted and when years of phone calls and letters failed, I turned left onto Highway 264, climbed First and Second Mesa, turned over rocks in Polocca until I found the woman who taught us how to count to ten. I knelt to kiss her weathered feet, cried into her lap, she shuffled over her dirt floor, fed me potatoes and boiled some coffee, ran her hands over my hair short as corn silk she knew I was deep in grief. I told her I ran after the Greyhound that took you south but that I could not call you back, asked how she got you into grandma's car that afternoon in Winslow decades ago, for the words she whispered in your ear. She said she was much younger then, but told me to show you the quiet things only sisters know, to place honey packets in your palms and pockets, to find a juniper and set down some stones for you—

So here we are in the orange light of 19th and Thunderbird, 464 miles from home. I will give you a minute. I will go through the boxes, the bags to find you a jacket. I will buy the cigarettes, the honey, hold your shaking hands through the fever, bring you spring water and call you teapot to slow down your heart. We can count the minnows. We can wait it out.

We can string these moments from old clotheslines when all of this is over. We can watch them weather and rust, call them pictographs and charge tourists five dollars to see them. We can argue about how it all happened. We can slam doors and meet again over boiling tea; we can borrow each other's clothes. We can learn how to grow old, how to watch where we are walking and to take our medicines, we can pretend it's getting young again. We can go to Nakai hall to watch young people fall in love to country songs and, somehow, the dirt clouds this love kicks up, the cowboy hats floating in soft, dance lights will make us remember—You made your own sundial with crochet needles and a paper plate, once, you were able to catch light.

Radio

Grandma sat in the back-most room.

The room caught the trailer's heat, the strongest signal. We unfolded chairs, stacked cardboard boxes, squeezed our smaller-selves into the blanket-draped places—used crochet needles as microphones, pretended to be country stars. At times, we opened our arms to fly— shirts lifted, us spinning, showing our white bellies just as the hawks did in our rectangle of the sky.

We loved the language spilling from AM radio, *All Navajo All the Time* and everything animal-shaped. We crawled on all fours, held our breath until we turned blue. We peeked through moth and mouse holes in the blankets, watched her stitch landscapes, palominos into pillowcases. We learned the mountain songs, her shuffle, traced the patterns her skirt left in floor-dust, hummed to the sound of plastic lids peeling off plastic boxes—crawled until she caught our legs, pulled us against her while she cleaned our ears, blew the dead skin off the bobby pins—held us until she was sure her girls were listening.

First, there was only a little static, a small snow. We were able to ignore it—collected restaurant suckers and made pictures with pushpins, listened to old country and trucks kick up dust on the road, waited for new seasons. Sweat crawled down our temples, broke apart on shoulders and knees, stirring her from sleep. She asked for the names of family places, Bitter Springs and Red Mesa, listened closely, brown paper eyelids opened behind yellowed lenses to make sure her girls were too.

She yelled at small storms, trains, blamed the static on lost satellites. She said that it was getting worse, but we heard voices and words the same—*Turn where white marks are carved into the edge.* We rearranged furniture and dusted antennas, stood on the trailer's roof and raised our arms, mimicked telephone poles and radio towers, changed batteries, ran aluminum up corners, along the ceiling.

She made us take down the clubhouse, keep our bellies covered. *I can't clean up after you girls anymore* and we unbraided our hair.

We stopped searching for glass beads and buttons and started counting coughs, pink fingers just under her nose to make sure she was still breathing.

We clung to everything we knew through the static. *Bingo.* Room. *Táláwosh.* Star. Hospital and North. A deep snow covered the satellites, and we thought of words we used to say.

Red Lights

With hands wrapped around a motionless steering wheel,

all white-knuckled and near shaking,

dad pressed his polished boot into the brake,

stomped with the other too near

the gas pedal I wondered

what places he had to get to,

what sort of business my hometown's neon offers white-

collared men, wondered

why he chose to stay here.

At this standstill, we watched

a group dance across the street,

move a gold, liquid sun between bandaged and

rope-burnt hands.

One man tipped the bottleneck toward a headlight-lit

wound, we watched gold

fill the purple reservoir

splitting his cheek in two I watched a tooth

fall, my dad shake his head, heard him mutter while I

traced the man's cross country build, this figure

with my fingers, wondered

which distance he ran in his youth, the six

mile muddied path behind the truck stops,

or the thirty mile run from Zuni into town

I recognized a face beneath one hood,

her profile like lightning I once traced

the initials needle-dotted behind

her ear in junior high, studied its pattern when she moved

this curtain, this rivering

of long black hair I

thought of canyon's watermarks, hoped

the fading letters belonged to her grandmother's name or

a scripture similar to that I

watched her throw her head back in laughter,

that same hair shining with traffic light—I

wished them a safe place to sleep—

wished for them to head home soon.

I wished for the red light to switch to green.

I hoped this hiss heard between the stomping was something
in the car,

not my father's muttering, hoped it was

the engine rattling—

or an animal even,

a snake or cottontail my dad found, maybe

one he injured or caught on the hike we were coming from.

I asked him if he counted the rooms of Chaco Canyon,
to tell me of swamplands, his childhood—
but didn't care if he counted,
didn't care how many of Pueblo Bonito's rock rooms opened
for the Southwest's deep purple sky I
believed in their secrets, but didn't want to hear his hissing,
or about the animals he placed in coffee cans,
didn't want to picture them coiled and uncoiling
themselves to shake grinds out of scales,
didn't want to know how long they lived
outside the reeds and waterways they were pulled from—
But this thought of water,
of sun-warmed bellies, the winding pattern snakes leave in
river sand
led me to think of the weekend before,
how softly this fighter from the valley said he had things to
show me,
the precision with which he pulled a pocketknife
from a pressed shirt pocket to cut
an apple still green and bruised
with wild into crescents—

how softly he placed the pieces on my tongue,

hands shaking as if he were going to break

them with his calloused, barbed-wire cut hands, softly as if

they were moon-shaped gems pulled straight from the sky—

And with these same hands he showed me how to throw

punches at ghosts by the river, how to get an enemy

to the ground, the ways you twist

their bodies around your chest, he threw

me over his shoulder to run his hands up the Achilles,

from the curves of the calf up and up—

And from this riverbank he led me to a one-bedroom house

to meet his grandfather,

to sit on the bed they still shared

and asked me to read to him, to them, to stop—

to repeat the words like *cedar* and *meadow*, *cicada*.

Cicada, cicada, their voices rang out after mine I

told them we believed the iron-shelled,

winged insects shielded the people from arrows when we

were moving up, up into this shining world, the grandfather

said *Yes. I think I've seen those scars—*

My father pressed the gas at the click of the lights—

asked why I asked about abandoned canyons

I said I remembered reading about something, or maybe I
told him that I was only curious
never telling him I was hungry,
that I have always been hungry for a green light, for home,
for people who learn lessons from streets
from fists or from horses—

That I've always been afraid he doesn't have a song in him,

no sweet, sweet notes to cover that hissing in his throat.

What We Found in the South Fork Puerco River

After Joy Harjo's *Grace*

Whiskey and the old, secret ways it unbridles men and women. All black hair and rodeo shirts pulled loose behind washing machines or road signs thrown out years ago. Still, we visit over coffee and talk of that tameless summer—fires juniper-tall and backpacks stuffed with singing cans—how the horses broke themselves into blackbirds running off mesas of clinging April snow—

How the body pattern of the one forgotten and left drunk in the filling wash crushed our Red Willow dreams and we decided we couldn't stay around the old homestead no more. So, we left that summer house to our mothers and knowledge of home inside the cinderblock-built frames of our memory and walked barefoot into Gallup or Grants. Walking their paved runoffs flooding with brown Puerco water, we searched for a new, shiny home.

Like wild people, we lost love for clay, the empty seats of pickup trucks and male rain caught in washbasins. So, we chased down everything that glittered—sparks from trains grinding against rail-lines and the burning side of cigarettes. We ran as the animals crawled under rocks to sleep, until vacancy signs warmed our bellies and frost burned our feet. And, in April, we stretched with first thunder to throw out hibernation and welcome a new spring. And we laughed because we felt new. And behind the Hacienda Hotel, knee deep in oily runoff water and with our hands parallel to telephone lines, we felt like we finally found home.

I wish I could say this new home was hugging a soft, brown woman with a homemade apron pulled tight around her waist, that all her waiting was over. Or talking about a red snake circling inside a crow. But there, on the concrete above the runoff, home was only a few minutes of comfort. We clicked our tongues to call horses down from the sky and remembered spring once meant walking barefoot down muddy dirt roads and hawks crossing silent, midday suns.

I want to say, with good intention, we hitch-hiked the hungry Highway 491 home. But we stayed in that hotel room three more neon-warm seasons. One January, you caught the last Greyhound to Santa Fe to sell road sign paintings or strands of obsidian beads and I walked toward Albuquerque or Phoenix or somewhere deeper South. Oh, how whiskey and shiny things still make us crazy.

Dispatches to Jupiter or Andromeda
or Some Other Place

Today, I feel snowpack melting,

like these words are sun-warm and strong

enough to reach you.

Somewhere, in the old, discarded encyclopedias I read out

loud to you when we were kids,

we learned that this land was an ancient, shallow sea.

You said, once, when I told you to be careful, that our bones

are sandstone and abalone,

our blood, pure-quartz sand.

But anyway, as I speak, a sandhill crane steps into a river,

gold and rippling with sun.

A sandhill crane steps into the gold river—

hands weave baskets in a house.

The basket-makers always smell of freshwater and reed.

They sing along to country radio as their hands work the wet
strips of willow into a circle.

They sing along to country radio as their hands work the wet
strips of willow into stairs,

steps signifying the paths to rainbows,

or to mountains.

Sometimes, I call the rainbows or mountains

the stairs lead to your

new home.

The basket-makers drive from Sanostee to Gallup to sell the basket made of reeds to my mom.

They meet in the littered parking lot of Safeway for the exchange.

My mom gives extra, *For gas money, diapers.*

The basket-maker inhales the air of it, this extra gift, eyes closed, smiling.

My mom presents the basket made of reeds to her mother.

They inhale the river of it in unison just as generations of mothers and daughters have done before them.

Grandma places frequently worn jewelry, a two-dollar bill, pictures inside of this basket.

May my family always smell a river, even as they're in deserts
on the other side of the world, or in cities, or falling apart— may they
always be surrounded by mountains,
by medicine.

A golden eagle rests in a cottonwood tree.

I wish you could see it.

Adinídíín, a light.

Light-at-the-end-of-a-tunnel,

You Are My Sunshine sung by Johnny Cash,

I wish you could hear it,
I wish you could see it,
the silver sun on our skin,

reflecting in the rainbow skin of a

freshly caught trout.

Remember camping as children,

our grandmothers gossiping in the camp kitchen,

the radio-static on the long drive home.

Picture us outside, barefoot in a mountain creek,

a van moves over the pass, just under the clouds, drops

shatter on sand.

I remember you, first, in firelight.

I remember you, next, in black-and-white television light.

I remember you, then, in fluorescent boarding-school light,

your name scribbled in Sharpie on the tags of clothing,

the insides of socks—

Now, I see you one or two pictures, in pixels, I hear your laugh
in static.
A split in the willows, the drying of a mountain creek—

She's been home for two weeks.

She's outside pulling weeds.

She's good, for now.

She's having a food sale.

We haven't had a monsoon season in six years,
the mountain is a tinderbox.
She's somewhere in town.
The mountain is on fire.
She's somewhere in the Dakotas, last we heard, while men
sing for the family in the house.
They pull hide over the floor,
your hands,
your hands always smelled like Cucumber Melon.
Your first-grade picture on the wall,

braids running down, down it

past the frame.

I call you hardened mud for what the trailer you were born in

stood on.

I call you caldera for when you grew bored, restless.

Once, they say, there was violent shaking, a tower of smoke,
ash, debris—
This violent eruption so hard to picture as we look over a
verdant blanket of grass.

Velvet elk move through it.

Imagine using their velvet bodies as pillows.

Twin fawns,
two constellations.
I imagine this valley of grass as your bed—
you are sleeping.

Someone asks how you are doing,

I see flashes, how our desert came to be.

I see floods and figures of people rippling in the distance like
gods.

Rain bloom at the bases of pillars.

Silver minnows in rock pools. Canyons widening.

The drops on the slick backs of clicking beetles.

People weeping on the edges of canyons,

dropping to their knees in the greenery of an oasis—

I'd look in every dark corner of downtown to

find you.

When we were just 12 and 14, you told me how you'd put

quarters in a sock to swing it into faces of enemies

to protect yourself,

you and your blood of quartz.

Sometimes, there you were,

in the boarding school visiting area, examining a bag full of

snacks or in a house

off Coors,

your shirt blood-splattered, mascara running—

every time,

you could walk on your own, nodded and said,

I'm okay.

I think of the bodies and tissues of small animals,

the children given away or lost walking to a relative's house to

find food.

All the small animals run into the rocks at the vibration of a

boot, at the sounds of vehicles and a world that keeps

moving.

You ran from sirens, from help.

We kept trying, offered you water like you were a wild horse.

At times, you were home, and well, for days, even months.

You sat with your children, showed them your cellphone
photography collection.
The endless water and evergreens and buffalo from up North,
you liked the wolf-printed blanket the most, loved to sketch
them when your hands were steady enough to fill in the eyes.

What kind of animals do they have up in the North country?

Wolves, grizzlies, horses—

all the color of ash or of sand.

These animals you loved are the ones unable to stay still,

I imagine them watching you through the evergreens as you
told us you were
working, that you'd be home in a few months, that you were
okay—
I see us, young, hear you begging me to go Trick-or-Treating
when, at ten, I felt too old.

You had those plastic vampire teeth,
our grandma sewed us last-minute capes.

Our favorite relatives healthy, coffee boiling over an open fire

at dawn, our grandmothers stopping by yard sales to buy

armfuls of books, encyclopedias,

how I'd give anything to go back there, now.

To that costume-cape and bad shade of purple Halloween

lipstick I hated, to hunting you down, calling hospital

and county jail lines—

I'm wondering, always wondering what it takes to make

someone leaving to look back,

to turn around,

to come home,

to allow all the animals inside of them

to rest.

Flood

It was New Year's Eve. Someone played an old country song our parents loved, their parents loved, I sang the psalms of the brokenhearted toward a jet-black night. Hail water crawled down those red canyon walls, the crests of coal horses. I said, *I don't drink this much. You're supposed to take care of me. My grandmother sang to fevered infants in hospitals. She took care of me.* Quilts, skirts, cedar beads wrapped around a wrist, afternoon t.v.—I sank into the warm wings of her, squeezed into the narrow, dusty openings of memory.

There are ten-thousand ways a desert can gut you; ten-thousand ways water finds the smallest openings to create a crack in the stone, a flash flood. She knew her heart was weakening. A snake rattles, hidden, in the brush. A blue jay lands on a man who fell asleep in the snow. I slept as you pressed your best shirts, packed a duffel. I watched you step onto a Greyhound headed to Prescott or somewhere south— headphones in, Cash singing that old country song our parents loved, their parents loved, listening with your head hanging low—

Love, I waited for your call, watched dust glitter in sunbeams, searched for star maps in letters you wrote. I found your father, met him for coffee in Holbrook. He received and kept the postcard you sent from Las Vegas years ago. I drove deeper into desert, searched every bus station in Phoenix, glanced at each doormat for a boot-print of Halchita red, red. They heard a clicking in my heart once, said that I cried with each heavy rain. They told me to stop crying, to never chase after a man, to splash walls with herb-water, to never keep his things around. A weakening. A flash, a flood, an absence. A horse's heart, a red stone beating.

I kept the boots you left by the door; white linoleum stained with a vermillion dirt. Spring-water runs red through the canyons. It's been years since that new year. The desert flashes in lightning-light—a juniper, white shells, swallows, the coal horses flash their teeth. Love, I've learned that my grandmother loved a man—I imagine him riding up on a dark horse, stirring the quail, walking up to the one-room house in a flower-printed, pearl-button shirt. I see her pouring him coffee, hair curled, jet-black and shining, each willow opening with the desert's breathing. *What did he do, where was he from, where did he go? He was from Utah, where red towers touch the blue, blue sky. He stopped coming around. We did not ask her about him. We heard he drowned in a mountain lake many years ago.*

Love, I still imagine jumping into the Pacific, the Colorado with you. I still see her waiting, watching the hills for a break in the landscape, for a dark horse. I imagine you in a desert deeper than this one, pensive, somewhere. I see you sitting in the short shade of a cedar tree. There are ten-thousand ways the desert can gut you; ten-thousand ways water finds the smallest openings to create a crack in the stone, a flash flood. You never looked at me and sang that old country song our parents loved; their parents loved—we never slow-danced in a one-room house.

I Dream of Taking You to Red Willow Valley

When we visit Red Willow Valley, we can put our arms around
sagebrush and hug the grey, branchy clouds of them.
I can use them to show you how we hugged our big uncles—
show you how they sat at slot machines, pretended to be in
Vegas with their 64 oz. coffee mugs, their pearl-buttoned
shirts.
I can show you how they fished or how they prayed,
mountain smoke snaking into the shapes of 7s.
We can recite the prayers they said for luck or to get the
saddles out of pawn,
their faces all lit and shining, grey rivering in the strands of
their low ponytails, the oil stains on the handkerchiefs draped
around their sunned necks.

I can show you how they sat on tailgates, sharpening knives
and laughing
when we asked if we were really born in Tombstone,
Arizona—
if our fathers were really White cowboys, Wyatt Earps or
John Waynes
like grandma said when she was angry about an uncleaned
kitchen, bottles she found hidden in the woodpile

or pawing a bracelet to make a cousin's bail—

Or I can tell you the lies I told to younger cousins about
where to find quail,

pearl-colored and proud with blue crowns wrapped tightly
around their feathered heads,

how I watched them search in the wrong places as I traced
their worn trail near the rusted propane tank with my toes in
secret.

I can tell you how I followed footpaths, how one led to the
front of the grey bobcat's den where I imagined he sat snake-
eyed, waiting for the sun to find sleep in the sea.

I imagined he dreamt of night just like my aunties
or young mother did as they sat in pickups
learning red lipstick and the sadness in Stevie Nicks' snow-
covered hills,
all hairspray, chipped nail polish
and pulling jeans over the brown
and soft rolling landscapes of them.

I can tell you that Red Willow Valley caught road dirt in her
wide-sky apron and poured its fine grains into our braided
hair during spring,

that hawks once nested in our woodshed.

We searched for peace while staring at their eyes like wet,
black moons,
searched like my cousins and I did when we went back after
years of living in town
to throw a party,
but I can tell you that the woodshed was not alive like I
remembered it, no longer churchlike
with eyas as idols or the place where our older cousins hid
those boarding schoolboys from Window Rock
like holding their hands or letting them undo their hair in its
thin strips of sun
was for worship or marks of their faith.
We went back thinking everything would be the same.

But, with absence, Red Willow became just a place outside of
town.

It allowed us to throw bottles and fight, to wake the wandering
rust-colored cows dreaming beneath a sky cracking open,
releasing its stars.

And under God or something like him or her or them,
drawing starlines across the long Southwest horizon,
my cousin poured our favorite whiskey onto the red, red sand.
*Out of remembrance, for this place and all that it was, the people we
loved and lost* she said,

and I could hear the quail pulling sage leaves off those
branches
one by one somewhere to the left of the old woodshed
and a crow with that animal-clicking in his throat, a rattle
started in the sage,
and I felt like the place came back to life then, more alive
than the steel sun,
more alive than the moon, than us after a few hours in town,
more than the truck
we drove from Gallup to get there and maybe it was even
more alive than the quail—
picking up our cigarette butts and bottle tops with their tiny
beaks to return to their nests with gifts.
I imagine them saying, *I went away*
but I'm back now.

You know, months later, I can still hear quail scattering like
those stars did and maybe still do.
So sometimes I keep my windows open.
And sometimes I keep the faucet running or all the lights on
because now I can,
because I want to show the horses electricity or how easy
water comes and because my cousin works at the gas station
and I at the same casino we waited outside of until 4 or 6 a.m.
for our uncles or mothers—

Because now we can celebrate,

we can pay for running water and the gas to drive

anywhere—Scattering House, Canyonlands, maybe California

or Vegas or maybe we can pick up a six pack and meet you

in Ya ta Hey or at the Junction if you're coming in from

Chinle.

But this time, I will tell you that sometimes, more than

swimming pools or electricity

or you in that dusty shirt you bought at the gas station in

Flagstaff,

I dream of going back and this time, staying.

So, maybe, if you'll live with me in Red Willow Valley,

we will fill our days with hauling water and sifting through

sand for seashells,

reciting stories of my childhood, my grandmother and uncle,

and I'll be all dreamy-eyed

like the auntie my cousins and I watched hold hands with the

chapter house janitor we called Chewy and I'll tell you about

the time we stretched on top of the woodshed

to watch him unbutton her waist-high disco jeans in its

shadow and wrap her hair around his rough hands like they

were magic and I'll say,

Maybe his hands were magic.

Maybe her neck was, too, because that afternoon

his cowboy hat and the soft sound rolling from her mouth

made us believe in love—

in Waylon, in talkin' about the good times

and all the good times yet to come,

in the stories coming out of grandma's radio, in the desert,

in boys and quail and everything ever brought into this valley—

all thirst and country music and a seven-people-to-one-room house and

that sky-apron catching horses and the sterling sun and all of our

red, red beating hearts.

Notes

"Radio"

The line "All Navajo, All the Time" is from KTNN-The Voice of the Navajo Nation radio's advertisement.

"What We Found in the South Fork Puerco River"

This poem was written after Joy Harjo's poem, "Grace."

"That Time I Dreamt I Took You to Red Willow Valley"

The line "...talking about the good times and the good times yet to come" are found in the lyrics of

Waylon Jennings' song "Good Hearted Woman"

The image "snow-covered hills" is found in "Landslide," a song by Fleetwood Mac.

Acknowledgments

Ahéhee', thank you, to the editors of the following journals for publishing the following poems, some of which were in their earliest drafts:

Narrative: "All-American Biography"

Literary Hub: "At the Red Lights," "Radio," and "January 31ˢᵗ, 1991"

Zocalo Press: "From 20 Miles Outside of Gallup, Holbrook, Winslow, Farmington, or Albuquerque
Terrain.org: "Sites"

Yellow Medicine Review: "Sun Dagger"

Connotation Press: "Away from Home," "Because you Are Magic, I Refuse to Admit the Last Place I Saw Her"

Contra Viento: "Flood"

The Dine Reader: "At Mention of Moab"

About the Author

Paige Buffington is Navajo, of the Naashashi (Bear Clan), born for the Biligaanaa (White People). Her grandparent clans are Ashiihi (Salt) and Biligaanaa. Her family is originally from Tohatchi N.M., a town sitting at the base of the Chuska Mountains in Navajoland. She received an MFA in poetry from the Institute of American Indian Arts in 2015. Hashtags accompanying her poems have included "American West," "memory," "family," and "desert Southwest." Her poems can be found in *The Dine Reader, Narrative Magazine, Honey Literary,* and *Contra Viento*, among others. Her poem "From 20 Miles Outside of Gallup, Holbrook, Winslow, Farmington, or Albuquerque" was awarded the 2023 Zocalo Public Square Poetry Prize. Her essay, "What Are You Looking For?" was selected as a finalist for the 2024 Waterston Desert Writing Prize. Her essay, "Restless" was named the winner of Prism International's Creative Nonfiction Contest. She currently lives in Gallup, N.M. She teaches Kindergarten near the Rock Springs, Yatahey, and China Springs communities on the Navajo Nations.

About the Press

Middle Creek Publishing & Audio is a company seeking to make the world a better place through both the means and ends of publishing. We are publishers of quality literature in any genre from authors and artists, both seasoned and those who are undiscovered or under-valued, or under-represented, with a great interest in works which illuminate or embody any aspect of contemplative Human Ecology, defined as the relationship between humans and their natural, social, and built environments.

Middle Creek Publishing & Audio's particular interest in Human Ecology is meant to clarify an aspect of the quality in the works we will consider for publication and as a guide to those considering submitting work to us. Our interest is in publishing works which illuminate the human experience through words, story or other content that connects us to each other, our environment, our history, and our potential deeply and more consciously.

In 2024, we are transitioning to Middle Creek Press, an NTEE A33: Arts, Culture, and Humanities - Printing and Publishing nonprofit organization. This change will empower us to focus more on the quality of our work and extend our literary reach. Be part of this transformative journey by supporting our fundraising efforts. If you have a moment, fill out the questionnaire on the following page or drop us a line at editor@middlecreekpublishing.com to give us feedback on our impact that we can use in grants reporting.

www.ingramcontent.com/pod-product-compliance
Lightning Source LLC
Chambersburg PA
CBHW061524050726
47503CB00016B/2718